0

The rights of Max Velthuijs to be identified as the author and illustrator of this work have been asserted by him in
accordance with the Copyright, Designs and Patents Act, 1988.

This paperback edition published in 1994 by Andersen Press.
First published in Great Britain in 1992 by Andersen Press Ltd., 20 Vauxhall Bridge Road, London SW1V 2SA. Published
in Australia by Random House Australia Pty., 20 Alfred Street, Milsons Point, Sydney, NSW 2061. All rights reserved.
Colour separated in Switzerland by Photolitho AG, Offsetreproduktionen, Gossau, Zürich. Printed and bound in Italy by
Grafiche AZ, Verona.

10   9   8   7   6   5

British Library Cataloguing in Publication Data available.

ISBN 0 86264 521 2

This book has been printed on acid-free paper

Max Velthuijs
Frog in Winter

Andersen Press · London

When Frog got up one morning, he realised at once that
something was wrong with the world. Something had
changed.

He went to the window and was astonished to see that everything was completely white.

He rushed outside in confusion. There was snow everywhere. It was slippery under his feet. Suddenly he felt himself falling over backwards...

...down the bank, into the river. But the river was frozen and Frog lay on his back on the cold, hard ice.
"If there's no water, I won't be able to wash," he thought, shocked.

Shivering with cold he sat on the bank. Then Duck came
hurrying towards him on her skates. "Hello Frog," she said.
"Nice weather today! Are you coming skating?"

"No, I'm freezing," replied Frog.
"But skating is good for you," said Duck. "I'll teach you."

So Duck gave Frog her skates and her scarf. She pushed him and he slid quickly across the ice, but not for long. Soon, he fell.

"Aren't you enjoying yourself?" said Duck. But Frog was nearly frozen solid and his teeth were chattering.

"You've got a warm feathery coat, but I'm just a bare frog," he said.
"You're right," said Duck, "you'd better keep my scarf, as I must be on my way."

Then Pig appeared with a basket of firewood on his back.
"Aren't you freezing Pig?" asked Frog.
"Freezing?" said Pig. "No, I'm enjoying the fresh, healthy air.
Winter is the most beautiful season."

"You have a nice layer of fat to keep you warm. But what do I have?"
"Poor Frog," thought Pig. "I wish I could help him."

One, two! One, two! Hare ran up. He was jogging in the snow.
"Hurrah!" he called joyously. "Sport makes you healthy! Hurrah for sport! Three cheers for sport!"

"Why don't you join in Frog? It's great fun keeping fit.
"I'm freezing," said Frog. "You've got warm fur, but I have
nothing." Sadly, he went home.

The next day his friends invited him to have a snowball fight.
But Frog couldn't share in the fun.

"I'm freezing," he murmured. "I'm only a bare frog," and
miserably he stumbled home.

He sat next to the fire for the rest of the day, dreaming of spring and summer. He burned every last piece of wood.

When the fire went out he went outside to gather more logs,
but he couldn't find any wood in the snow.

He walked and walked until he lost his way. Everything was white. Exhausted he lay down in the snow. A bare frog.

And there his friends found him.
"I'm freezing," whispered Frog.
"Come on," said Hare, and carefully they carried him home
and put him to bed.

Hare collected wood and lit a fire. Pig cooked a nourishing soup and Duck cheered Frog up.

In the evenings, everyone listened while Hare read
wonderful stories about spring and summer. Meanwhile, Pig
knitted Frog a warm pullover in two colours. Frog enjoyed
the attention from his friends. Winter is wonderful when you
can spend it in bed!

Then the day came when Frog was well enough to get up.
Without fur, fat or feathers, but dressed in his new pullover,
he took his first steps in the snow.
"Well?" asked Hare curiously.
"It's good," answered Frog bravely.

So the long winter passed. But one morning when Frog opened his eyes he noticed at once that something was different. Bright light streamed in the window. Quickly, he jumped out of bed and ran outside.

The world was bright green and the sun shone in the sky.
"Hurray!" he cried. "It's good to be a frog. How wonderful.
I can feel the sun's rays on my bare back."
His friends were happy to see Frog so cheerful.

"What would we do without Frog?" laughed Hare.
"I can't think," said Pig.
"No," agreed Duck, "life just wouldn't be the same without
him."

Andersen Press paperback picture books

FRANKIE MAKES A FRIEND
by Tony Bradman & Sonia Holleyman

SCRUMPY
by Elizabeth Dale & Frédéric Joos

EMERGENCY MOUSE
by Bernard Stone & Ralph Steadman

FROG IN WINTER
by Max Velthuijs

FROG AND THE STRANGER
by Max Velthuijs

FROG IS FRIGHTENED
by Max Velthuijs

THE GREAT GREEN MOUSE DISASTER
by Martin Waddell & Philippe Dupasquier

THE TALE OF GEORGIE GRUB
by Jeanne Willis & Margaret Chamberlain

THE TALE OF MUCKY MABEL
by Jeanne Willis & Margaret Chamberlain